SUP
LUCKY DIP

Written by Lesley Young
Based on characters created
by Mike Young

Carnival

An Imprint of HarperCollins *Publishers*

SuperTed and Spotty were in their tree house, deep in a secret forest.

"Sizzling strawberries!" said SuperTed. "It's so hot! I've got to cool off."

"I know!" said Spotty. "I'll make my special spotty sundae."

"But it's only Tuesday," said SuperTed, mopping his face with the back of his paw.

"Not that kind of Sunday!" said Spotty. "I mean vanilla ice-cream with lots of juicy cherries."

"I've got a better idea," said SuperTed. "Let's find a swimming pool." He went over to the video screen and pressed some buttons.

"What are you looking for?" asked Spotty.

"Wait and see," said SuperTed.

Up on the screen came a picture of a white building with a large square hole in its roof.

"Great moons of Spot!" said Spotty. "Where's the roof? Has a storm blown it off?"

"It's meant to be like that," said SuperTed. "It's an open-air swimming pool – just what we need to cool off."

"It looks wonderful," said Spotty. "But why is it empty? Where is everyone?"

SuperTed pressed a button and the picture on the screen grew bigger. Now Spotty could see children standing round the pool. They were holding their towels over their shoulders and shivering. One of them dropped an apple on to the surface of the pool and it bounced.

"Spotted sputniks!" gasped Spotty, "Hard water!"

"That's ice," said SuperTed. "There must be something wrong. Let's see if we can help."

He whispered his secret magic word to himself and changed in a moment from an ordinary teddy bear into SuperTed.

"Strap on your rocket pack," he said to Spotty, "and follow me."

They both shot out of the tree house and flew straight to the swimming pool.

"SuperTed and Spotty!" shouted the children when they saw them. "Our pool has turned into ice. Can you help us?"

Just then they heard a horrible cackle from one of the changing rooms. In the gap under the swing door they could see a pair of boots and a pair of flippers.

"Rocketing rhubarb!" said SuperTed. "It's Dr Freezing Frost and Pengy the Penguin Man!"

The door flew open and out burst Dr Frost.

"Why aren't you at your ice-cream fortress at the South Pole?" asked SuperTed.

Dr Frost laughed and everyone shivered. "I ran out of pools of water for my experiments," he hissed, "so I thought I'd use this one."

"I suppose we could try skating," said Spotty.

"But we want to swim!" shouted the children.

"I just like splashing about and having fun," said a very small child with water wings.

"Don't worry," said SuperTed, "we'll make ripples for you. Come on, Spotty!"

And to everyone's surprise, he shot off through the hole in the roof.

High in the sky, on a cloud, Mother Nature was busy stuffing pillow cases with rainbows.

"SuperTed! And Spotty!" she smiled when she saw them. "Would you like one of these pillows? It would give you happy dreams!"

"We're in the middle of a nightmare just now," said SuperTed, "But I know you can help."

The two friends told Mother Nature what had happened at the pool.

"So Dr Freezing Frost's up to his evil tricks again," she tutted. "Just show me where this frozen pool is."

Far below, Dr Frost and Pengy were sliding up and down on the ice.

"We gave SuperTed the cold shoulder," cackled Dr Frost. "That's the last we'll see of him, the bothersome bear!"

The two villains began to make
pictures in the ice with their feet.
Mother Nature leaned over the edge
of her cloud and sprinkled a handful
of magic dust over the frozen pool.

Suddenly a burst of rain came
through the open roof.

"That's funny," said Pengy. "It's
raining, but the sun's shining!"

Dr Frost put out his hand, and then he shook all over. "This rain is hot! You know I can't stand heat – get me out of here!"

The hot rain hit the ice and hundreds of small holes appeared. For a moment the ice looked like a sieve, then the holes all joined up as the ice melted.

"Oh no!" shrieked Dr Freezing Frost.
"We're in hot water!"

He and Pengy splashed out of the
swimming pool. Then they whooshed
back to their ice-cream station
quicker than you could say "a double
ice-cream cone with chocolate flake
and raspberry sauce, please!"

The rain stopped and the children got
ready to jump in the pool. Just then a
rainbow appeared through the roof.
SuperTed and Spotty slid down it,
landing with a *SPLASH* in the water.

"Melting mangoes!" said SuperTed.
"Lovely cool water at last!"

SuperTed looked round at the children. "Before you jump in, can you all swim?" he asked.

Two small children shook their heads.

"Pulsating prunes! You shouldn't be near the deep end if you can't!" he cried. "You must all learn. But today I can give you a short cut."

He opened his paw and threw some of Mother Nature's magic dust over them.

"Now you can swim," he said, "so let's all enjoy ourselves."

Spotty splashed water up into the sunshine and laughed. "Life with SuperTed is always the best kind of lucky dip!"

SUPERTED SAYS
Keep safe in the water

NEVER

- go near water without an adult.
- go into deep water unless you can swim.
- go swimming straight after a meal.
- run around the sides of a swimming pool.
- jump in on top of other people.

Learn to swim and have lots of fun!